MUNSCH
Mini-Treasury Two

by Robert Munsch
art by Michael Martchenko

annick press

toronto • new york • vancouver

We acknowledge the support of the Canada Council for the Arts, the Ontario Arts Council, and the Government of Canada through the Book Publishing Industry Development Program (BPIDP) for our publishing activities.

ONTARIO ARTS COUNCIL
CONSEIL DES ARTS DE L'ONTARIO

Cataloging in Publication

Munsch, Robert N., 1945-
    Munsch mini-treasury. Two / by Robert N. Munsch ; art by Michael Martchenko.

Contents: Stephanie's ponytail — The fire station — I have to go! — Moira's birthday — Thomas' snowsuit.
ISBN 978-1-55451-274-4

      1. Children's stories, Canadian (English).
I. Martchenko, Michael II. Title.

PS8576.U575M8497 2010a   jC813'.54   C2010-902015-4

Distributed in Canada by:
Firefly Books Ltd.
66 Leek Crescent
Richmond Hill, ON
L4B 1H1

Published in the U.S.A. by Annick Press (U.S.) Ltd.
Distributed in the U.S.A. by:
Firefly Books (U.S.) Inc.
P.O. Box 1338
Ellicott Station
Buffalo, NY 14205

Printed and bound in China.

visit us at: **www.annickpress.com**
visit Robert Munsch at: **www.robertmunsch.com**

CONTENTS

Stephanie's Ponytail

Story by Robert Munsch
Art by Michael Martchenko

Stephanie's Ponytail came about in 1992 because one of Robert Munsch's friends, who was a student teacher, asked him to come to his class and tell stories. While he was there, Munsch tried making up some new stories. One of the kids who asked to be in a story was named Stephanie. She had a ponytail coming right out of the top of her head, so he made up a ponytail story for her. The class really liked it. Munsch decided this was a good one to turn into a book. Later, Munsch surprised Stephanie by just showing up one day at her school to give her copies of *Stephanie's Ponytail*. She said, "Never do that again. When I got called to the principal's office I thought I was in trouble!"

★ ★ ★

To Stephanie Caswell, Durham, Ontario
                            — *Bob Munsch*

One day Stephanie went to her mom and said, "None of the kids in my class have a ponytail. I want a nice ponytail coming right out the back."

So Stephanie's mom gave her a nice ponytail coming right out the back.

When Stephanie went to school, the other kids looked at her and said, "Ugly, ugly, *very* ugly."

Stephanie said, "It's *my ponytail* and *I* like it."

The next morning, when Stephanie went to school, all the other girls had ponytails coming out the back.

Stephanie looked at them and said, "You are all a bunch of copycats. You just do whatever I do. You don't have a brain in your heads."

The next morning the mom said, "Stephanie, would you like a ponytail coming out the back?"

Stephanie said, "No."

"Then that's that," said her mom. "That's the only place you can do ponytails."

"No, it's not," said Stephanie. "I want one coming out the side, just above my ear."

"Very strange," said the mom. "Are you sure that is what you want?"

"Yes," said Stephanie.

So her mom gave Stephanie a nice ponytail coming out right above her ear.

When she went to school, the other kids saw her and said, "Ugly, ugly, *very* ugly."

Stephanie said, "It's *my ponytail* and *I* like it."

The next morning, when Stephanie came to school, all the girls, and even some of the boys, had nice ponytails coming out just above their ears.

The next morning the mom said, "Stephanie, would you like a ponytail coming out the back?"

Stephanie said, "NNNO."

"Would you like one coming out the side?"

"NNNO!"

"Then that's that," said her mom. "There is no other place you can do ponytails."

"Yes, there is," said Stephanie. "I want one coming out of the top of my head like a tree."

"That's very, very strange," said her mom. "Are you sure that is what you want?"

"Yes," said Stephanie.

So her mom gave Stephanie a nice ponytail coming out of the top of her head like a tree. When Stephanie went to school, the other kids saw her and said, "Ugly, ugly, *very* ugly."

Stephanie said, "It's *my ponytail* and *I* like it."

The next day all of the girls and all of the boys had ponytails coming out the top. It looked like broccoli was growing out of their heads.

The next morning the mom said, "Stephanie, would you like a ponytail coming out the back?"

Stephanie said, "NNNO."

"Would you like one coming out the side?"

"NNNO!"

"Would you like one coming out the top?"

"NNNO!"

"Then that is definitely that," said the mom. "There is no other place you can do ponytails."

"Yes, there is," said Stephanie. "I want one coming out the front and hanging down in front of my nose."

"But nobody will know if you are coming or going," her mom said. "Are you sure that is what you want?"

"Yes," said Stephanie. So her mom gave Stephanie a nice ponytail coming out the front.

On the way to school she bumped into four trees, three cars, two houses and one Principal.

When she finally got to her class, the other kids saw her and said, "Ugly, ugly, *very* ugly."

Stephanie said, "It's *my ponytail* and *I* like it."

The next day all of the girls and all of the boys, and even the teacher, had ponytails coming out the front and hanging down in front of their noses. None of them could see where they were going. They bumped into the desks and they bumped into each other. They bumped into the walls and, by mistake, three girls went into the boys' bathroom.

Stephanie yelled, "You are a bunch of brainless copycats. You just do whatever I do. When I come tomorrow, I am going to have ... SHAVED MY HEAD!"

The first person to come the next day was the teacher. She had shaved her head and she was bald.

The next to come were the boys. They had shaved their heads and they were bald.

The next to come were the girls. They had shaved their heads and they were bald.

The last person to come was Stephanie, and she had ...

a nice little ponytail coming right out the back.

The Fire Station

by Robert Munsch
illustrations by Michael Martchenko

Where did This Story come from?

The Fire Station is another story that goes back to Robert Munsch's time as a teacher in a daycare center in Coos Bay, Oregon. The children in the story are based on a boy and girl in the daycare center who were always getting into trouble. For example, in the middle of one night, the boy got up and washed all the windows in his house—only he used bug spray instead of window cleaner. All the windows got very sticky. The children asked Munsch to make up a story about them, so he came up with the fire station story. In fact, the children in the daycare center often went to the fire station. The kids loved to sit on the front of the fire truck, so it made a great deal of sense that they should be in a story about a fire station.

★ ★ ★

To Holly Martchenko, Toronto, Ontario,
and to Michael Villamore and
Sheila Prescott, Coos Bay, Oregon

Michael and Sheila were walking down the street. As they passed the fire station Sheila said, "Michael! Let's go ride a fire truck."

"Well," said Michael, "I think maybe I should ask my mother, and I think maybe I should ask my father, and I think maybe..."

"I think we should go in," said Sheila. Then she grabbed Michael's hand and pulled him up to the door.

Sheila knocked: BLAM – BLAM – BLAM – BLAM – BLAM. A large fireman came out and asked, "What can I do for you?"

"Well," said Michael, "maybe you could show us a fire truck and hoses and rubber boots and ladders and all sorts of stuff like that."

"Certainly," said the fireman.

"And maybe," said Sheila, "you will let us drive a fire truck?"

"Certainly not," said the fireman.

They went in and looked at ladders and hoses and big rubber boots. Then they looked at little fire trucks and big fire trucks and enormous fire trucks. When they were done Michael said, "Let's go."

"Right," said Sheila. "Let's go into the enormous fire truck."

While they were in the truck, the fire alarm went off: CLANG – CLANG – CLANG – CLANG – CLANG.

"Oh, no!" said Michael.

"Oh, yes!" said Sheila. Then she grabbed Michael and pulled him into the back seat.

Firemen came running from all over. They slid down poles and ran down stairs. Then they jumped onto the truck and drove off. The firemen didn't look in the back seat. Michael and Sheila were in the back seat.

They came to an enormous fire. Lots of yucky-colored smoke got all over everything. It colored Michael yellow, green and blue. It colored Sheila purple, green and yellow.

When the fire chief saw them he said, "What are you doing here!"

Sheila said, "We came in the fire truck. We thought maybe it was a bus. We thought maybe it was a taxi. We thought maybe it was an elevator. We thought maybe..."

"I think maybe I'd better take you home," said the fire chief. He put Michael and Sheila in his car and drove them away.

When Michael got home he knocked on the door. His mother opened it and said, "You messy boy! You can't come in and play with Michael! You're too dirty." She slammed the door right in Michael's face.

"My own mother," said Michael. "She didn't even know me." He knocked on the door again.

His mother opened the door and said, "You dirty boy! You can't come in and play with Michael. You're too dirty. You're absolutely filthy. You're a total mess. You're...Oh, my!...Oh, no!...YOU'RE MICHAEL!"

Michael went inside and lived in the bathtub for three days until he got clean.

When Sheila came home she knocked on the door. Her father opened it and saw an incredibly messy girl. He said, "You can't come in to play with Sheila. You're too dirty." He slammed the door right in her face.

"Ow," said Sheila. "My own father and he didn't even know me."

She kicked and pounded on the door as loudly as she could. Her father opened the door and said, "Now stop that racket, you dirty girl. You can't come in to play with Sheila. You're too dirty. You're absolutely filthy. You're a total mess. You're...Oh, my!...Oh, no!... YOU'RE SHEILA!"

"Right," said Sheila, "I went to a fire in the back of a fire truck and I got all smoky. I WASN'T EVEN SCARED."

Sheila went inside and lived in the bathtub for five days until she got clean.

Then Michael took Sheila on a walk past the police station. He told her, "If you ever take me in another fire truck, I am going to ask the police to put you in jail."

"JAIL!" yelled Sheila. "Let's go look at the jail! What a great idea!"

"Oh, no!" yelled Michael, and Sheila grabbed his hand and pulled him into the police station.

I HAVE TO GO!

by Robert Munsch
illustrated by Michael Martchenko

Where did This Story come from?

When Robert Munsch's son Andrew was almost three years old, he was still wetting his bed. One night, he wet the bed so many times that there were no more sheets; Munsch had to wash them in the middle of the night. The next day, Munsch was telling stories in a small town when a little boy in the front row started to jump up and down on his seat. After a while he started to yell, "pee, pee, pee!" His father ran down the aisle, carried him out the back door, brought him back in a few minutes, and sat him down. When Munsch asked, "Who wants to be in a new story?" the little kid who had to pee stuck up his hand and said, "me, me." His name was Andrew, the same name as Munsch's son. Very soon afterwards, the story *I Have to Go!* was made into a book.

★ ★ ★

To Andrew McIsaac of Cookstown, Ontario,
and to Andrew Munsch of Guelph, Ontario

One day Andrew's mother and father were taking him to see his grandma and grandpa. Before they put him in the car his mother said, "Andrew, do you have to go pee?"

Andrew said, "No, no, no, no, no."

His father said, very slowly and clearly, "Andrew, do you have to go pee?"

"No, no, no, no," said Andrew. "I have decided never to go pee again."

So they put Andrew into the car,
fastened his seatbelt and gave him lots of
books, and lots of toys, and lots of crayons,
and drove off down the road—VAROOMMM.
They had been driving for just one minute
when Andrew yelled, "I HAVE TO GO PEE!"

"YIKES," said the father.

"OH NO," said the mother.

Then the father said, "Now, Andrew, wait just five minutes. In five minutes we will come to a gas station where you can go pee."

Andrew said, "I have to go pee RIGHT NOW!"

So the mother stopped the car— SCREEEEECH. Andrew jumped out of the car and peed behind a bush.

When they got to Grandma and Grandpa's house, Andrew wanted to go out to play. It was snowing, and he needed a snowsuit. Before they put on the snowsuit, the mother and the father and the grandma and the grandpa all said, "ANDREW! DO YOU HAVE TO GO PEE?"

Andrew said, "No, no, no, no, no."

So they put on Andrew's snowsuit. It had five zippers, 10 buckles and 17 snaps. It took them half an hour to get the snowsuit on.

Andrew walked out into the backyard, threw one snowball and yelled, "I HAVE TO GO PEE."

The father and the mother and the grandma and the grandpa all ran outside, got Andrew out of the snowsuit and carried him to the bathroom.

When Andrew came back down they had a nice long dinner. Then it was time for Andrew to go to bed.

Before they put Andrew into bed, the mother and the father and the grandma and the grandpa all said, "ANDREW! DO YOU HAVE TO GO PEE?"

Andrew said, "No, no, no, no, no."

So his mother gave him a kiss, and his father gave him a kiss, and his grandma gave him a kiss, and his grandpa gave him a kiss.

"Just wait," said the mother, "he's going to yell and say he has to go pee."

"Oh," said the father, "he does it every night. It's driving me crazy."

The grandmother said, "I never had these problems with my children."

They waited for five minutes, 10 minutes, 15 minutes, 20 minutes.

The father said, "I think he is asleep."

The mother said, "Yes, I think he is asleep."

The grandmother said, "He is definitely asleep and he didn't yell and say he had to go pee."

Then Andrew said, "I wet my bed."

So the mother and the father and the grandma and the grandpa all changed Andrew's bed and Andrew's pajamas. Then the mother gave him a kiss, and the father gave him a kiss, and the grandma gave him a kiss, and the grandpa gave him a kiss, and the grownups all went downstairs.

They waited five minutes, 10 minutes, 15 minutes, 20 minutes, and from upstairs Andrew yelled, "GRANDPA, DO YOU HAVE TO GO PEE?"

And Grandpa said, "Why, yes, I think I do."

Andrew said, "Well, so do I."

So they both went to the bathroom and peed in the toilet, and Andrew did not wet his bed again that night, not even once.

MOIRA'S BIRTHDAY

Story by Robert Munsch
Art by Michael Martchenko

Where did This story come from?

Robert Munsch came up with the story *Moira's Birthday* at the end of a long tour in the Northwest Territories. He was staying with a family in Hay River. At the end of a day of storytelling he returned home, and there was their daughter Moira having her sixth birthday party. She wanted him to make up a story, which he did. Actually, Munsch doesn't like birthday parties very much, but he was happy to make up a story for the occasion. He remembered when his daughter Julie had invited a lot more kids to her party than her parents said she could have, so he pretended that Moira had asked the whole school to her party. As soon as he thought of the story, he said, "Hey, that's really good!"

★ ★ ★

To Moira Green

One day Moira went to her mother and said, "For my birthday I want to invite grade 1, grade 2, grade 3, grade 4, grade 5, grade 6, aaaaand kindergarten."

Her mother said, "Are you crazy? That's too many kids!"

So Moira went to her father and said, "For my birthday I want to invite grade 1, grade 2, grade 3, grade 4, grade 5, grade 6, aaaaand kindergarten."

Her father said, "Are you crazy? That's too many kids. For your birthday you can invite six kids, just six: 1-2-3-4-5-6; and NNNNNO kindergarten!"

So Moira went to school and invited six kids, but a friend who had not been invited came up and said, "Oh, Moira, couldn't I please, PLEASE, PLEEEASE COME TO YOUR BIRTHDAY PARTY?"

Moira said, "Ummmmmm ... OK."

By the end of the day Moira had invited grade 1, grade 2, grade 3, grade 4, grade 5, grade 6, aaaaand kindergarten. But she didn't tell her mother and father. She was afraid they might get upset.

On the day of the party someone knocked at the door: rap, rap, rap, rap, rap, rap. Moira opened it up and saw six kids. Her father said, "That's it, six kids. Now we can start the party."

Moira said, "Well, let's wait just one minute."

So they waited one minute and something knocked on the door like this:

blam, blam, blam, blam.

The father and mother opened the door and they saw grade 1, grade 2, grade 3, grade 4, grade 5, grade 6, aaaaand kindergarten. The kids ran in right over the father and mother.

When the father and mother got up off the floor, they saw: kids in the basement, kids in the living room, kids in the kitchen, kids in the bedrooms, kids in the bathroom, and kids on the ROOF!

They said, "Moira, how are we going to feed all these kids?"

Moira said, "Don't worry, I know what to do."

She went to the telephone and called a place that made pizzas. She said, "To my house please send two hundred pizzas."

The lady at the restaurant yelled, "TWO HUNDRED PIZZAS! ARE YOU CRAZY? TWO HUNDRED PIZZAS IS TOO MANY PIZZAS."

"Well, that is what I want," said Moira.

"We'll send ten," said the lady. "Just ten, ten is all we can send right now." Then she hung up.

Then Moira called a bakery. She said, "To my house please send two hundred birthday cakes."

The man at the bakery yelled, "TWO HUNDRED BIRTHDAY CAKES! ARE YOU CRAZY? THAT IS TOO MANY BIRTHDAY CAKES."

"Well, that is what I want," said Moira.

"We'll send ten," said the man. "Just ten, ten is all we can send right now." Then he hung up.

So a great big truck came and poured just ten pizzas into Moira's front yard. Another truck came and poured just ten birthday cakes into Moira's front yard. The kids looked at that pile of stuff and they all yelled, "FOOD!"

They opened their mouths as wide as they could and ate up all the pizzas and birthday cakes in just five seconds. Then they all yelled, "MORE FOOD!"

"Uh-oh," said the mother. "We need lots more food or there's not going to be a party at all. Who can get us more food, fast?"

The two hundred kids yelled, "WE WILL!" and ran out the door.

Moira waited for one hour, two hours, and three hours.

"They're not coming back," said the mother.
"They're not coming back," said the father.
"Wait and see," said Moira.
Then something knocked at the door, like this:

blam, blam, blam, blam.

The mother and father opened it up and the two hundred kids ran in carrying all sorts of food. There was fried goat, rolled oats, burnt toast, and artichokes; old cheese, baked fleas, boiled bats, and beans. There was eggnog, pork sog, simmered soup, and hot dogs; jam jars, dinosaurs, chocolate bars, and stew.

The two hundred kids ate the food in just ten minutes. When they finished eating, everyone gave Moira their presents. Moira looked around and saw presents in the bedrooms, presents in the bathroom, and presents on the roof.

"Uh-oh," said Moira. "The whole house is full of presents. Even I can't use that many presents."

"And who," asked the father, "is going to clean up the mess?"

"I have an idea," said Moira, and she yelled, "Anybody who helps to clean up gets to take home a present."

The two hundred kids cleaned up the house in just five minutes. Then each kid took a present and went out the door.

"Whew," said the mother. "I'm glad that's over."

"Whew," said the father. "I'm glad that's over."

"Uh-oh," said Moira. "I think I hear a truck."

A great big dump truck came and poured one hundred and ninety pizzas into Moira's front yard. The driver said, "Here's the rest of your pizzas."

Then another dump truck came and poured one hundred and ninety birthday cakes into Moira's front yard. The driver said, "Here's the rest of your birthday cakes."

"How," said the father, "are we going to get rid of all this food?"

"That's easy," said Moira. "We'll just have to do it again tomorrow and have another birthday party! Let's invite grade 1, grade 2, grade 3, grade 4, grade 5, grade 6, aaaaaaand kindergarten."

The End

THOMAS' SNOWSUIT

Story – Robert Munsch
Art – Michael Martchenko

Where did This story come from?

Robert Munsch was in Halifax, Nova Scotia, when he agreed to tell some stories to kids in daycare. All the daycare centers in Halifax were invited to come and hear him. When he walked into the room there were about 300 children from ages three to five. His first thought was, "Oh dear, am I supposed to keep them happy for an hour? I don't have enough stories." And sure enough, after 45 minutes, he had run out of stories. Then he noticed that all the kids were wearing snowsuits. That led to a story about a little boy named Thomas who didn't want to put on his snowsuit. The kids loved it because every time someone tried to put him into his snowsuit, Thomas yelled, "Noooooo," and all 300 kids would start yelling "Nooooo" as well.

To Otis and Erika Wein in Halifax,
who helped me make up this story,
and to Danny Munsch

One day, Thomas' mother bought him a nice new brown snowsuit. When Thomas saw that snowsuit he said, "That is the ugliest thing I have ever seen in my life. If you think that I am going to wear that ugly snowsuit, you are crazy!"

Thomas' mother said, "We will see about that."

The next day, when it was time to go to school, the mother said, "Thomas, please put on your snowsuit," and Thomas said, "NNNNNO."

His mother jumped up and down and said, "Thomas, put on that snowsuit!"

And Thomas said, "NNNNNO!"

So Thomas' mother picked up Thomas in one hand, picked up the snowsuit in the other hand, and she tried to stick them together. They had an enormous fight, and when it was done Thomas was in his snowsuit.

Thomas went off to school and hung up his snowsuit. When it was time to go outside, all the other kids jumped into their snowsuits and ran out the door. But not Thomas.

The teacher looked at Thomas and said, "Thomas, please put on your snowsuit."

Thomas said, "NNNNNO."

The teacher jumped up and down and said, "Thomas, put on that snowsuit."

And Thomas said, "NNNNNO."

So the teacher picked up Thomas in one hand, picked up the snowsuit in the other hand, and she tried to stick them together. They had an enormous fight, and when they were done the teacher was wearing Thomas' snowsuit and Thomas was wearing the teacher's dress.

When the teacher saw what she was wearing, she picked up Thomas in one hand and tried to get him back into his snowsuit. They had an enormous fight. When they were done, the snowsuit and the dress were tied into a great big knot on the floor and Thomas and the teacher were in their underclothes.

Just then the door opened, and in walked the principal. The teacher said, "It's Thomas. He won't put on his snowsuit."

The principal gave his very best
PRINCIPAL LOOK and said, "Thomas,
put on your snowsuit."

And Thomas said, "NNNNNO."

So the principal picked up Thomas in one hand and he picked up the teacher in the other hand, and he tried to get them back into their clothes. When he was done, the principal was wearing the teacher's dress, the teacher was wearing the principal's suit, and Thomas was still in his underwear.

Then from far out in the playground someone yelled, "Thomas, come and play!" Thomas ran across the room, jumped into his snowsuit, got his boots on in two seconds, and ran out the door.

The principal looked at the teacher and said, "Hey, you have on my suit. Take it off right now."

The teacher said, "Oh, no. You have on my dress. You take off my dress first."

Well, they argued and argued and argued, but neither one wanted to change first.

Finally, Thomas came in from recess. He looked at the principal and he looked at the teacher. Thomas picked up the principal in one hand. He picked up the teacher in the other hand. They had an enormous fight and Thomas got everybody back into their clothes.

The next day the principal quit his job and moved to Arizona, where nobody ever wears a snowsuit.

Books in the Munsch for Kids series:

The Dark
Mud Puddle
The Paper Bag Princess
The Boy in the Drawer
Jonathan Cleaned Up, Then He Heard a Sound
Murmel, Murmel, Murmel
Millicent and the Wind
Mortimer
The Fire Station
Angela's Airplane
David's Father
Thomas' Snowsuit
50 Below Zero
I Have to Go!
Moira's Birthday
A Promise is a Promise
Pigs
Something Good
Show and Tell
Purple, Green and Yellow
Wait and See
Where is Gah-Ning?
From Far Away
Stephanie's Ponytail
Munschworks
Munschworks 2
Munschworks 3
Munschworks 4
The Munschworks Grand Treasury
Munsch Mini-Treasury One
Munsch Mini-Treasury Two

For information on these titles please visit www.annickpress.com
Many Munsch titles are available in French and/or Spanish. Please
contact your favorite supplier.